Runaway Pony

MARGUERITE HENRY'S Misty Inn

Runaway Pony

By Kristin Earhart

Illustrated by Serena Geddes

ALADDIN

New York London Toronto Sydney New Delhi

This book is a work of fiction. Any references to historical events, real people, or real places are used fictitiously. Other names, characters, places, and events are products of the author's imagination, and any resemblance to actual events or places or persons, living or dead, is entirely coincidental.

ALADDIN

An imprint of Simon & Schuster Children's Publishing Division

1230 Avenue of the Americas, New York, New York 10020

First Aladdin paperback edition September 2015

Text copyright © 2015 by Estate of Marguerite Henry

Illustrations copyright © 2015 by Serena Geddes

Also available in an Aladdin hardcover edition.

All rights reserved, including the right of reproduction in whole or in part in any form.

ALADDIN is a trademark of Simon & Schuster, Inc., and related logo is a registered trademark of Simon & Schuster, Inc.

For information about special discounts for bulk purchases, please contact Simon & Schuster Special Sales at 1-866-506-1949 or business@simonandschuster.com.

The Simon & Schuster Speakers Bureau can bring authors to your live event. For more information or to book an event contact the Simon & Schuster Speakers Bureau at 1-866-248-3049 or visit our website at www.simonspeakers.com.

Designed by Laura Lyn DiSiena

The text of this book was set in Century Expanded.

Manufactured in the United States of America 1220 OFF

Library of Congress Control Number 2015945444

10 9 8 7 6 5 4

ISBN 978-1-4814-1420-3 (hc)

ISBN 978-1-4814-1419-7 (pbk)

ISBN 978-1-4814-1421-0 (eBook)

To Moochie and Wendy, thank you

Runaway Pony

Chapter 1

FULL MOON FANCY. THE NAME SOUNDED MAGICAL. Willa let the words swirl in her head. She couldn't believe there was a new pony at Miller Farm.

"Just Fancy for short," Grandma Edna insisted. "No need for long, frilly names around here." When Grandma said "here," she meant the animal rescue center she ran. It was home to goats, chickens, rabbits, and especially ponies—Chincoteague ponies.

Ben and Willa hurried over to the small paddock to meet Fancy. "Where is she?" Ben wondered, glancing at his big sister. Willa searched the field.

"The small pasture's empty, Grandma," Willa called across the yard.

Grandma looked up. Her scowl pushed her eyebrows low. She stood up from her rose-bushes. "Now don't tell me," she murmured. Grandma made her way over to where Willa and Ben stood. "Sure enough," she announced, examining the area. "We've got a pony to find. You two look on the other side of the house. I'll check behind the barn."

Before rushing off, Ben yanked a handful of

clover from the tall grass by the fence. "It's a peace offering," he said. "In case we find her." Willa nodded, amazed at how well her brother understood animals.

Even though Willa had taken riding lessons when they lived back in Chicago, she wouldn't have thought to grab a treat for the runaway pony. Ben had not really been around ponies or horses before they had moved to their new house on Chincoteague Island, but he had an easy way with them.

Now both kids were around horses and ponies every day. First, there was Buttercup. Buttercup belonged to their neighbors but was staying in the old barn at Ben and Willa's house for a while. Second, there were the horses at Grandma and Grandpa's place, Miller Farm. Of all those ponies, Willa and Ben shared a favorite: a sweet buckskin mare named Starbuck. Starbuck had arrived at the rescue center earlier that summer. At the time, her leg had been hurt. The kids had helped nurse Starbuck back to health, and now they loved her like their own.

But they couldn't think about Starbuck now. They had a lost pony to find!

"Grandma sounded mad," Ben remarked as they raced past the barn and the big pasture.

"She's probably just worried," Willa said as she rounded the corner of the one-story farmhouse. The grassy part of the yard was small but there was a deep wooded area in the back.

"We don't even know what Fancy looks like," Ben commented.

"Well, she's the one that's just roaming around, not in the pasture," Willa replied, swatting a bug away from her freckled nose. She squinted as she scanned the yard and trees. "I don't see her. Let's go to the garden."

Ben trudged behind his sister, glancing back over his shoulder. If he were a pony, where would he hide?

No luck in the garden. All they found was their grandma.

"I thought she'd be here too," Grandma Edna said. "It'd be just like that pony to make a feast of my carrots."

"Hey! What's going on?"

They looked up to see Lena and Clifton heading their way. Clifton was a teenager and often helped on the farm. His younger sister, Lena, sometimes tagged along. Willa was excited to see her friend.

"Lena, you have to help. There's a pony missing!" As Willa shared the details, Lena listened closely, twirling a finger around one of her many beaded braids.

"Let's first look for clues," Lena announced as soon as Willa was done. Together, Lena, Willa, and Ben went back to the small pasture. Clifton took the path through the woods. Grandma ran inside to recruit Grandpa. They would follow the fence along the far side of the barn, down toward the beach.

Lena moved quickly, but she did not rush. She carefully walked around the outside of the paddock fence. Next, she checked the closed gate and its latch. "Evidence!" she called out when she noticed a pile of manure.

"It's still steaming," Ben noted, his nose crinkled.

"That means it's fresh. Fancy can't have gone far," Lena determined. She shielded her eyes from the late-morning sun and turned a full circle. Willa and Ben searched too.

Willa frowned. It didn't make sense. Where was that new pony? If she couldn't have gone far, why hadn't they found her?

"Who's that?" Ben asked, pointing into the larger pasture area.

Willa's gaze fell on an unfamiliar pony, a shiny bay with a bushy mane and tail. The pony was standing right next to Starbuck. She had her head down and was busy ripping up tiny bites of grass.

Just then Grandma and Grandpa hurried out the farmhouse door. Grandpa had his keys, and Grandma held a lead rope.

"Grandma!" Willa called. "Is that her? Is that Fancy, grazing by Starbuck?"

"Well, I'll be," Grandma exclaimed. "How on earth did that mare find her way in there?"

It was a good question, but neither Grandma nor Grandpa attempted to answer it. Instead, they immediately headed for the gate and began to fiddle with the latch.

Willa, Ben, and Lena watched, confused.

"Do you think your grandma forgot she put Fancy in the main pasture?" Lena questioned.

"I doubt it," Willa answered. "Grandma never forgets anything."

"Especially not about the animals," Ben added. Grandma Edna had been a vet, and she prided herself in taking the best possible care of each and every creature at Miller Farm.

"Well, the fence looks too high for a pony to just jump over, and your grandparents are acting strange," Lena said. "I think there's something special about that new pony."

Willa knew Lena loved a mystery. Lena would turn anything into a whodunit, just so she could investigate. But, this time, Willa suspected her friend might be right.

"Let's go see what they're looking at," Lena suggested. The kids approached the entrance to the pasture quietly, curiously.

"What are you three doing here?" Grandma asked as soon as she noticed them. "Why don't you go for a walk down by the beach?"

Willa and Ben were happy to take their grandmother's suggestion. They loved to explore by the ocean, but even after they had arrived at the beach, Lena was certain they had been chased away on purpose. "Your grandparents are hiding something," she insisted.

"Don't be silly, Lena," Willa replied, curling

her long toes into the wet sand. "My grandparents have nothing to hide. They only want to take good care of the ponies." Willa was sure of that.

By the time their parents came to pick them up at the end of the day, Willa and Ben hardly remembered the earlier excitement of the escaped pony. The new excitement was that Dad was meeting Starbuck for the first time.

"So this is the pony I've heard so much about," Mr. Dunlap said. With a gentle nudge, Mom encouraged him to reach out his hand. Ben quickly put an apple slice on his dad's palm. After a few warm sniffs, Starbuck took the treat and crunched it happily. Dad had grown up in the city, so he didn't have much experience with horses.

"Isn't she great?" Willa asked, looking into the pony's warm brown eyes.

"She seems nice enough," Dad admitted.

"Starbuck's the best," Ben said, and he gave her another apple slice.

Chapter 2

BEN'S GOOD MOOD HAD DISAPPEARED BY THE
next day. "When does school start?" he mumbled.
When Ben was grumpy, all his words came
out low and rumbly, running together.

"Next Tuesday," Mom answered as she
pulled into a parking spot in front of Seacoast
Elementary. "Aren't you excited?" Mom's
voice was high and chirpy. Willa wondered if

their mom was most excited of all.

Everyone got out and closed their doors. "This is exactly how they did it when I was a student here," Mom explained. "They would post the class lists on the front windows of the school." Willa and Ben rushed forward, but Mom lingered on the edge of the sidewalk.

Willa spotted the sheet for fifth grade immediately. As soon as she found her name, she scanned farther down the roster. Sarah Starling! Lena Wise!

"Willa!"

Willa turned around when she heard her name. "Sarah!" she yelled back to her friend, who had just arrived. "We're in the same class. Lena, too."

Sarah grabbed Willa's hand and pulled her

back to the windows to survey the list.

"Mr. McGory! He's supernice, and he has lots of animals in his room." Sarah gave Willa's hand a happy squeeze. Only then did the two delighted girls notice their less-than-thrilled brothers standing next to them.

Ben and Sarah's brother, Chipper, shared the same dismal expression. They did not have the same teacher.

"I got Ms. Hardy," Chipper moaned. He turned to Ben. "In case you wondered, her name fits her. She is *not* easy. You have Ms. Freeman. She is nice *and* funny."

"At least you'll know someone in your class," Ben complained back. "You are the only person I know in the whole school."

"Um, exaggerate much?" Sarah asked.

"You kind of know your sister . . . and me."

Ben's face scrunched up. Big sisters—and their friends—didn't count. Ben scooted closer to Chipper. Then he started whispering.

The moms had been talking near the parking lot, but they came toward the school entrance now.

"What are you two up to?" Mom asked with a coy expression when she saw Ben and Chipper.

"Nothing." The boys answered so quickly they gave themselves away. They were concocting a plan.

"Nothing big at least," Ben added.

The moms looked at each other and smiled.

"I like when school starts again," Mrs. Starling said.

"Me too," Willa and Ben's mom added. "Once

the kids are in class, I can get organized and really think about the inn."

"Your bed-and-breakfast!" Mrs. Starling exclaimed. "When's the grand opening?"

The Dunlaps had a big, old house, and they planned to use the extra bedrooms for guests— paying guests. There would be a restaurant, too.

"Not for a while," Mom admitted. It was taking longer than they had thought. "We just finished the website. We put it up so we could feel like the inn is a real thing, but we're still a far cry from being ready for business. Maybe later this fall."

Willa was listening to the parents' conversation. "Later this fall" sounded far away. Summer had been so nice, so carefree. No school, no real routine. Willa liked school, but she wished things didn't have to change.

"No way!"

Willa had never heard Mom use that phrase before. She exchanged glances with Ben between bites of spaghetti. They were the only ones at the big wooden dinner table. Mom and Dad claimed they were too distracted to eat.

"No way!" Mom repeated.

"You're the one who wanted to put up the website," Dad said, shaking his head. "You said it would make the inn seem 'real.'"

"I didn't think someone would book a room in the first twenty-four hours." Mom was pacing now, striding from one side of the kitchen island to the other. She stared at the laptop on the counter. She glared at it as if it were a bully who had played a mean trick.

Dad slouched on a stool and watched Mom go back and forth. His eyebrows were up, but the corners of his mouth turned down.

"It's so soon!" Mom continued. "We still need to paint the downstairs bathroom, and clean out all that stuff behind the barn."

Willa and Ben looked at each other. Mom was just getting started. She always rattled off long lists of things to do. "And put up towel hooks, and—"

"We can do this," Dad announced, interrupting the list.

"We can?" Mom questioned.

"Of course," Dad said, slapping his hand on the counter. He was sitting up nice and straight now. "It's just one weekend. We don't need to have the restaurant up and running. We don't have to have every detail in place."

"You're right," Mom replied. "Just the one room, and then a nice breakfast."

"Yes. A bed and a breakfast," Dad confirmed. "That's it."

Mom and Dad both sighed.

Willa and Ben both took deep breaths. To them, it sounded like a lot.

Chapter 3

"I'M NOT SURE YOU'RE OLD ENOUGH FOR THAT,"
Mom said, putting a stack of dirty breakfast
dishes in the sink. It was the next day, and
Willa was trying to make the most of the end of
summer vacation.

"But it would be so much fun," Willa
insisted. "Maybe Grandma would let Sarah
ride Fancy; then we could take a picnic down

to the dunes. I'll bet Starbuck would love it."

"It sounds lovely, but I don't think your grandma would let you girls go off on your own with two ponies, especially two ponies she doesn't know that well. Grandma would feel too responsible if something went wrong."

"What could go wrong?" As soon as the words slipped out of her mouth, Willa wanted to take them back. She knew you could not plan for everything, especially when animals were involved.

"Besides, you can't just go off and leave your brother."

"Ben could hang out with Chipper," Willa suggested. "He doesn't like to ride as much as I do." Willa was pretty sure of that. Ben seemed to enjoy just being *around* the animals.

She noticed a pad of paper on the table across from her. "What's this?" she asked, reaching for it.

"It's our to-do list," Mom answered.

"Wow, you actually wrote it all down," Willa commented. "Instead of just announcing everything at dinner. That's good, Mom." Willa had always believed in lists herself.

"Yes, if we are going to have other people in our home, we have to get serious, get organized," Mom said. "For starters, you and your brother can't leave your stuff down here."

"Okay," Willa said.

"It has to go in your room, first thing after you get home from school."

That made sense. "I'll make sure Ben does it too."

"Great. Your dad and I really need your help."

"Okay," Willa said again. She wasn't sure how their conversation had changed. It had started with her talking about taking ponies for a picnic on the beach, and it had ended with Mom handing her and Ben a basket of clean clothes to put away and talk of even more chores. Summer was definitely coming to an end.

"Really?" Ben asked when Willa passed on the news later that day. He kicked the toe of his sneaker in the sandy driveway dirt. "We never had to keep our school stuff in our rooms in Chicago."

"We never ran an inn in Chicago either."

Ben turned toward the old white house. He looked way up to where the guest rooms were, on the third floor. "Do you really think Mom and Dad can do this?"

Willa looked up too, her eyes squinting against the sun. "Yes, I do. Mom made a real list this time. On paper."

Ben's eyebrows shot up. A real list.

"And they didn't give us any crazy jobs, like cleaning out all the weeds behind the barn. We got easy chores, like being in charge of Amos after school."

"But what about all our other chores? Will we still be able to go to Miller Farm?" Ben asked.

Willa bit her lip. She was worried about that too. They had to make it to the farm to visit Starbuck.

Willa and Ben had taken on a number of chores over the summer. They helped care for Buttercup by cleaning her stall. They were responsible for feeding Amos, the adorable black-and-white puppy who was Buttercup's best friend. Willa and Ben also took care of New

Cat, who was in charge of mouse control. There were other jobs that didn't have anything to do with animals, but those were not nearly as much fun. Those jobs did, however, take time. "We'll have to do our chores first thing when we get home, then head straight to the farm. And we'll have to take Amos with us."

"If we take Amos, we have to walk. That'll take *forever*! He's always sniffing." Ben was right, the puppy hardly took three steps without stopping to smell something.

"I have a plan," Willa reassured him.

For the next half hour, Willa and Ben searched through the barn for supplies. Mom and Dad used part of the old red barn for storage. Plus, there were lots of things left from the previous owners. The kids had spent a lot of time in the

Our To-do List

Buttercup

- ☐ Clean stalls
- ☐ Brush
- ☐ Fresh Hay
- ☐ Water
- ☐ Paddock morning

Amos

- ☐ Food
- ☐ Walk & play ball
- ☐ Puppy training

New Cat

- ☐ Food
- ☐ Water
- ☐ Chin Scratch

building. They were the ones who had cleared out the stalls, just in case. Thanks to them, Buttercup was able to come stay at Misty Inn when he had become sick. Buttercup was great, but there were two stalls, and Willa and Ben hoped that one day the other one would belong to a certain special pony.

"I couldn't find a straw basket," Ben told Willa. "Only this old crate."

"That's fine. This isn't *The Wizard of Oz*," Willa said, examining the plastic crate to check the size. "We just need some cardboard on the bottom so his legs don't poke through."

"And a blanket, so he's comfy. Or he'll jump out."

Willa studied her brother's face. She thought it was funny that he could think of that, but he couldn't remember to put on clean underwear unless someone told him.

"Look! I'll bet this crate was used as a bike basket before." Willa pointed to where a bracket and some screws hung from one of the crate's corners. That setup made it easier. Willa held the crate in place while Ben tightened the screws.

All the hard work was worthwhile. Amos loved the crate. As soon as Ben plopped him inside, he smelled the soft green blanket and woofed happily. Then, when Willa put her weight on the bike pedals and started riding, Amos placed his front paws on the edge and yipped for joy. Willa pedaled as carefully as she could. It was hard not to laugh, the way Amos's tongue dangled from his mouth.

"That's one problem solved," Willa announced after their quick ride around the neighborhood. "Now we can take Amos with us when we go to the farm."

"So we can still see Starbuck," Ben concluded. "Good."

It was good. Their grandmother was very practical about the ponies at the rescue center. Starbuck's leg was totally healed. The pony didn't need to stay at the rescue center anymore. If Grandma Edna decided it was time to find Starbuck a new home, Grandma would do it. When she made up her mind, that was that. But the Dunlap kids wouldn't give up their favorite pony without a fight.

Chapter 4

"I DON'T KNOW HOW I FORGOT ABOUT IT," MOM said, sounding concerned, nervous, and guilty all at once.

"Don't worry, Mom. We'll be fine." Willa handed her mother a notebook, which she placed in her small suitcase. It was the Friday before school started, and Mom had remembered just the day before that she had to go on a trip.

"I signed up for this bed-and-breakfast conference months ago. I had no idea I'd miss your first day of school." She looked up at Willa as she zipped her bag. "Sorry, sweetie."

"It's fine. There will be lots of school days," Willa said.

"When did you get so grown-up?" Mom asked. She sounded sad.

Willa was the most organized one in the family. Everyone knew that, so it wasn't a surprise that Mom had told her she'd need to help Dad. "You know he's not good at getting you guys out the door in the morning," she said.

"Don't worry," Willa assured her.

"Make sure you and Ben are ready for the bus. Be at the mailbox by eight o' clock."

"We will be," Willa assured her again. They

heard the doorbell. "That must be Grandma."

"She's always early," Mom said. "Especially for the airport." She tugged her bag behind her.

Everyone came down to see Mom off. She gave them all hugs. "Take care of one another," she ordered. "And no more tardies."

Mom looked right at Willa when she said that.

Willa elbowed Ben.

Dad just smiled. "Learn lots about bed-and-breakfasts," he said. "Our guests will be here before you know it."

Mom blew a kiss and ducked into the car. Grandma Edna waved and backed out of the driveway.

"What should we do now?" Dad asked blankly.

Willa sighed. She was going to be busy while Mom was gone.

On the morning of the first day of school, Willa woke to a horrible clanging. "Did Dad get a new alarm?" she mumbled as she pushed herself out of bed. The clanging grew louder. The house seemed to rattle and shake. Willa stumbled out of her room and followed the sound. It led her upstairs, to one of the guest bedrooms. Her dad was there, kneeling in front of an old metal contraption, which was hissing.

"What's going on?" Willa cried over the noise.

"I think the radiator is broken," he said. "It got cold last night, so I turned on the heat."

A spray of steam sputtered from the pipe. "Watch out!" Dad yelled. "It could burn you."

They stood at a distance and stared at the noisy, drippy, feisty radiator.

"No showers this morning," Dad announced. "This is an old house, and I think the heat and the plumbing are connected."

"All right," Willa said, heading downstairs to wake Ben, who had managed to sleep through the racket.

"You should avoid all plumbing," Dad called from the third floor. "Don't even use the sink."

The morning routine was tricky without running water. Willa and Ben had to brush their teeth with water from the pitcher in the fridge. Willa used that to wash off the apples for their lunches too. Things took longer. Before they knew it, they were running late for the bus.

"Hurry!" Willa insisted, zipping her lunch box.

Ben grabbed his backpack and rushed to the door.

Dad appeared at the top of the stairs with a mop and a bucket. A stream dribbled down from the top step. "Have a great first day, kids!" He was smiling and looking hopeful, despite his soggy pajama pants.

"Do you need help?" Willa asked. "Should we stay?"

"No. Everything will be fine," he said. He held the mop up straight with one hand and saluted with the other.

Willa laughed as she took Ben's hand and ran out the door. They could see the bus from the front porch. "Go!" Willa yelled, and Ben leaped ahead. He made it to the mailbox just as the yellow bus's door folded open. Willa came up behind him. By the time Chipper and Sarah got on at the next stop, Willa had caught her breath.

Sarah slid in beside her. Chipper sat with Ben. Willa sighed. They had made it! Even without Mom. Even with a crazy radiator leak. Even without running water. She was relieved . . . and certain the rest of the day would be a breeze after that.

Then the bus jolted to a stop.

"Well, I never," the bus driver proclaimed. He scratched his graying whiskers and stared out the front window.

Sarah stood up to look out. "Oh no!" she exclaimed. "Willa!"

As soon as Willa stood up, she gulped.

There, in the middle of the road, was Starbuck.

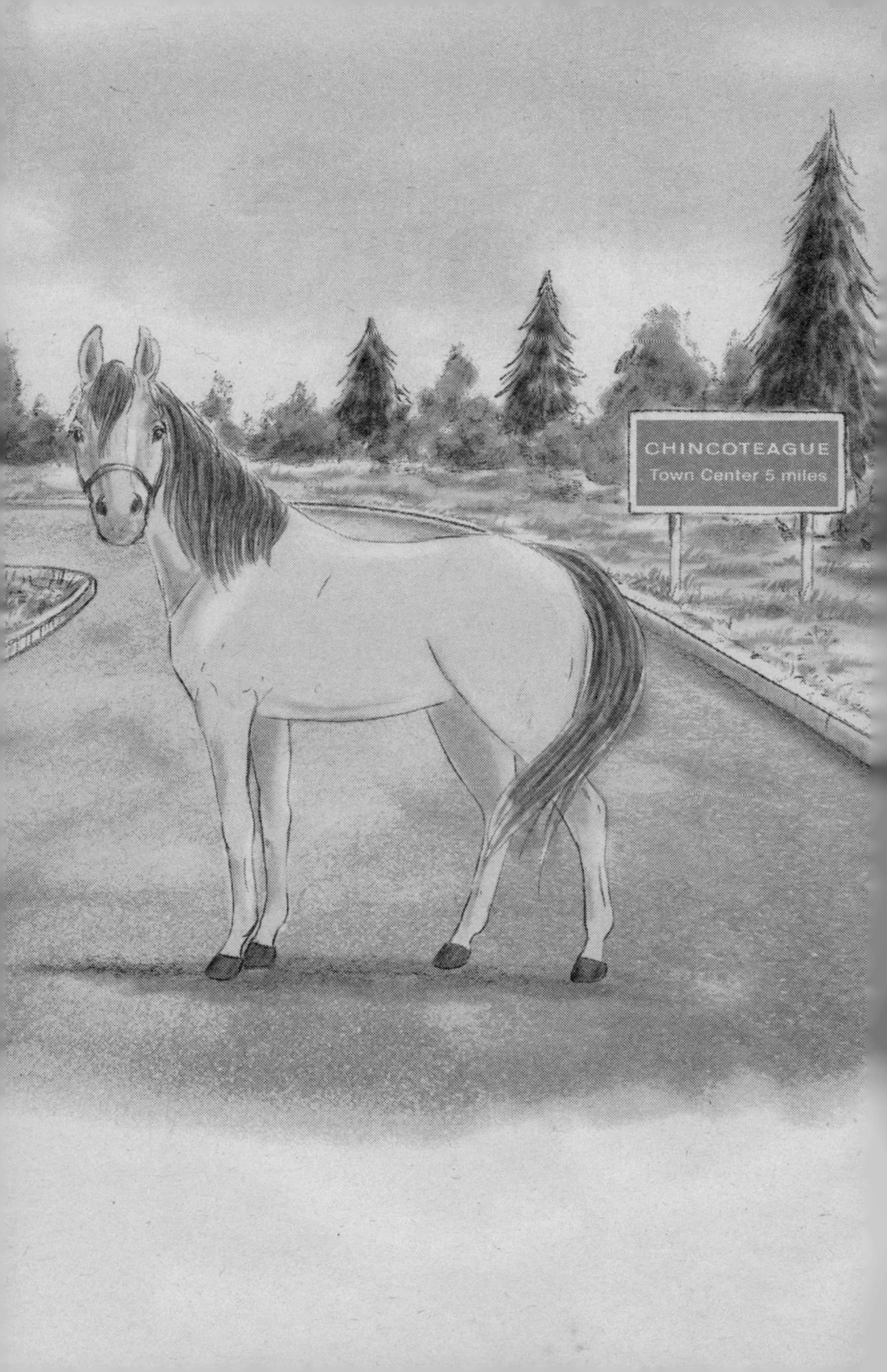
CHINCOTEAGUE
Town Center 5 miles

Chapter 5

WILLA RACED TO THE FRONT OF THE BUS. "I know that pony. I have to get off," she declared.

"Nothing doing, missy," the bus driver said. "I can't let anyone off. Only at school or your stop. It's a rule."

"But someone might hit her. She could get hurt."

Now Ben was standing next to her. "Please, mister," he begged.

"I'm sorry, but it's my job to get you to school safely," he said. "Can't let no runaway pony get in the way." The bus driver leaned his head and shoulder out the narrow window. "Move along now," he called.

The buckskin pony did not move, so he honked the horn.

"Starbuck, get out of the road. It's not safe," Willa pleaded, though not loud enough for her favorite pony to hear.

The bus driver honked again. All the kids on the bus were now standing and yelling.

For a moment Starbuck stood her ground. She seemed unfazed. She faced the bus head-on, lazily flicking an ear and swishing her tail.

"Go on, girl," Willa whispered.

Starbuck pricked her ears forward. She tossed her head in the air and whinnied. Then, slowly, she made her way to the side of the road and stopped there.

"That's a good horse," the bus driver said, easing the bus back into gear.

Willa and Ben scurried to the back row of seats and watched out the window. Starbuck didn't move. She just got smaller as the bus drove away. Brother and sister pushed themselves against the glass to catch the last glimpse of her. Willa felt trapped. They had to do something! How had Starbuck gotten out? Where was she going? And how would she get back home?

"I've got my walkie-talkie," Ben said hopefully, but then he remembered Chipper had the other one in the front of the bus. It was part of their master plan to keep in touch, even though they had different teachers.

"We couldn't have used it to call Dad anyway," Willa said, flopping around to sit down. "The house is flooding."

Sarah was waiting at the bus door. As soon as Willa stepped to the ground, Sarah's hand was on her shoulder. "We'll go straight to the office. Ms. Parker will help us."

Willa told Ben to go with Chipper, so the other boy could show him where his class would be. "I promise to let you know as soon as I hear anything." She bent down to look into her brother's eyes. He nodded, but didn't say a word.

Sarah led Willa into the office of Seacoast Elementary. It looked a lot like the office at

Willa's old school in Chicago. Willa had gone there whenever she was late and had to check in.

A woman with cat earrings and long, hot-pink-painted fingernails looked up from the front desk. "Sarah Starling," she said. "Welcome back."

Sarah smiled, introduced Ms. Parker to Willa, and explained the situation. When Sarah was done, Ms. Parker sent her on to class. Willa looked at the clock. It was already 8:18. School started at 8:20. She had given Mom her word: no more tardies.

"Don't you worry," Ms. Parker said. "I'll take you to class. Your teacher won't count you late." She picked up a phone with a long curly cord. "Go ahead and call your grandma. She'll know just what to do."

When Willa hung up the phone, she felt a little better. Grandma Edna was leaving right away to track down Starbuck. She had said she'd call Sarah's mom to help too.

"Your grandma is something else," Ms. Parker said. "My Patsy refuses to go to any other vet." When Willa looked closer at Ms. Parker's desk, she noticed a collection of picture frames. All featured photos of a large black-and-white cat.

"Grandma's pretty great," Willa agreed.

Ms. Parker told stories about Patsy as she walked Willa to class. When Willa opened the door to Room 24, all heads turned to her. Normally, Willa would have been embarrassed, but she quickly located Sarah's and Lena's friendly faces. She forced a smile when Mr. McGory pointed to an empty desk. She sat down and tried to pay attention, but she could not stop thinking about Starbuck.

Just before lunch, there was a knock on the classroom door. It was Ms. Parker. She had a piece of folded pink paper in her hand. "A message for Willa Dunlap," she said.

Whispers flitted all around as Willa opened the note.

Your grandma called to say Starbuck is safe back at Miller Farm. You can visit her later. I let your brother know too.
Ms. P.

She had drawn a cat face next to her name.

♥

Starbuck's escape was big news at the lunch table. "It's not a coincidence," Lena insisted.

"What does that mean?" Sarah asked as she opened her sandwich tin.

"Two ponies and two escapes in two weeks?" Lena said, waving her pretzel rod in the air. "They have to be connected. I suspect foul play."

"You always suspect foul play," Sarah retorted.

"I agree that it's weird," Willa said. She was still too nervous to eat. "But I don't think anyone is letting them loose on purpose."

"Maybe not," Lena admitted. "But why do you think Starbuck wandered so far from the farm? The other pony didn't do that."

Willa had been wondering the same thing.

"Maybe Starbuck wants to be free," Sarah suggested, "to go back to Assateague."

Willa turned to her friend, horrified. She never would have thought of that. The very idea hurt Willa's feelings.

Sarah didn't seem to notice. "Remember how Phantom, Misty's mother, swam back to Assateague to be with the wild herd?"

Of course Willa remembered. Willa had read the famous book about Misty several times by now. She was fascinated by the fact that wild ponies lived on Assateague Island, a thin sliver of land that lay between Chincoteague and the open sea. "But Phantom had been wild for a long time," Willa argued. "Starbuck hasn't lived on Assateague since she was a foal. Her old owners told us so."

Sarah shrugged. "It looked like she was going somewhere. I was just trying to figure out where."

Willa didn't have a reply. She was so fond of Starbuck. She wanted the pony to be happy. Willa hoped she wasn't running away from Miller Farm.

Chapter 6

IT HARDLY FELT LIKE THE SAME DAY WHEN they arrived home after school. They soon found their dad on the third floor. Willa was relieved that he wasn't still in his pajamas, but his jeans and T-shirt were sopping wet.

"How was your day?" he asked.

"Anything but typical," Willa said. Ben agreed with a firm nod of his head.

"Mine was about the same," Dad replied. "Homework?"

"A little," Willa replied. "I can do it after dinner." Ben nodded again.

"What did you think about the other kids? Did you meet anyone new?"

"Kind of," Willa answered. A picture of Ms. Parker, with her nails and old-fashioned phone, popped into her head. But the secretary wasn't a kid! "I mostly hung out with Sarah and Lena."

"Ben?" Dad asked.

"Same," was Ben's answer. Willa noticed his hand move to touch the walkie-talkie hanging from his belt. She felt bad that Ben and Chipper weren't in homeroom together. It wasn't easy making brand-new friends.

Even though Willa had been nervous about

the first day—new school, new kids, new challenges—that had all gone smoothly compared to the Great Starbuck Escape fiasco.

Willa noticed a stack of dry rags right next to a pile of wet ones.

"Do you need help?" she offered, even though she had hoped they'd be able to go to the farm.

"Not really," Dad said, surveying the puddle that surrounded the radiator. "Your grandfather came by with one of his friends who is a plumber. He fixed the leak. I just have to clean up now." He sloshed the mop back in a rubber bucket. "Besides, I think you two might want to check in on that pony Starbuck. I'm sure you want to get the rest of the story from Grandma."

"Yes, yes!" Willa's face brightened. She reached to hug her dad with both arms, but he tried to pull away.

"I'm all wet, sweetheart," he said. "You've got your good school clothes on." Willa squeezed tighter. She was sometimes surprised how adults didn't think about what really mattered. Her clothes could always go in the wash.

♥

Dad fixed them a huge after-the-first-day-of-school snack. They filled him in on the thrilling bus ride and all the events that had followed. He gave them a play-by-play of how the radiator sounded when it started to spout water like a fountain. Ben almost choked on his cheese and crackers. Their dad could be pretty silly when he wanted.

"You sure you have enough energy to ride to your grandparents'?" Dad asked.

Willa and Ben were sure. Amos was too. The puppy yipped happily as Ben placed him in the carrier on the front of Willa's bike. Ben lingered there, scratching Amos behind the ears. "You think she's okay?"

It took Willa a moment to realize what her brother was asking. "Starbuck is fine," she answered. "Grandma would have let us known if something had happened. She'd have told Grandpa to tell Dad, then Dad would have told us." Willa knew that much for certain, but she had other concerns. What if Starbuck was trying to get free, like Sarah had said? What if Grandma decided the beautiful buckskin was too much trouble and needed to go to a new home right away? Willa didn't have answers to those questions, so she rode her very fastest to Miller Farm. Ben struggled to keep up.

When they arrived, Starbuck trotted over right away. The pony looked as good as new. Maybe better.

Willa lifted Amos from the crate, and the puppy waddled right into the field. He touched noses with Starbuck, his tail wagging like a windup toy. Then he moved on to make friends with Fancy. He ran between the two ponies, making figure eights, stopping from time to time to give them each a sniff. He often did the same thing to Buttercup, back home.

Ben reached his arm over the top rail of the wooden fence and stroked Starbuck's velvety ears. The pony's eyelids fluttered closed. She looked peaceful. "Maybe she wasn't trying to run away," Ben suggested. "Maybe she was trying to find us."

Willa took a deep breath and gazed at her little brother. She had been thinking the same thing—hoping the same thing—but she didn't dare put the thought into words.

"I think she could track us down," Ben continued. "I think she's that smart."

All of a sudden, Grandma Edna was right behind them. She had appeared out of nowhere. "Smart? There's nothing smart about getting loose. Starbuck could have been hit by a car out there. The road is never a safe place for a horse, and it was rush hour."

Willa had to hide her smirk. Compared to the city, Chincoteague had no rush hour on its roads. But she still got Grandma's point. They were lucky Starbuck was back at Miller Farm, safe and sound. "Thank you, Grandma," Willa said. "For going to get her. We were so worried."

"I was worried too. It was definitely out of character for that pony."

As they spoke, Fancy ambled up next to Starbuck. Fancy gave a low nicker of greeting to Starbuck. Starbuck nickered back to the shiny bay. Then Fancy put her head over the fence, hoping to get a pet as well.

"Now, Starbuck, you'd best be careful in choosing your companions," Grandma advised. Willa recognized that tone. It had a hint of disapproval. Willa wondered what Grandma Edna

was trying to say. Did she question whether Starbuck and Fancy should be friends? That seemed odd. Ben was glancing back and forth, from Grandma to the two ponies. He was trying to figure it out as well.

Willa told herself that it couldn't hurt to ask. "What do you mean, Grandma?"

"I mean that we can't have Starbuck picking up any bad habits. Especially not now. She's good and healthy again, so we should be finding her a new home." Grandma stepped forward and gave Starbuck a steady pat on the neck. "You be good now, you hear?" she said to the buckskin pony.

Hearing Grandma mention a new home for Starbuck rattled Willa. She was so flustered that she barely heard what Grandma said next.

It was something about how Grandpa had driven to the hardware store to buy a new latch for the pasture gate. "Can't have any more escape antics," she murmured as she headed to the barn.

It was hard to settle down and think about homework after all the excitement of the day. Even though they were in different classes and different grades, Willa and Ben had the same assignment. They had to write a personal essay about what they had done during the summer. So much had happened! Where would they even start?

Chapter 7

A FEW DAYS PASSED WITHOUT ANY DRAMA AT the Dunlap house. Both kids made it to the bus stop on time, and the bus didn't make any unexpected stops for animals in the middle of the road. The radiator in the upstairs bedroom was fixed, and everyone could take showers again. Mom came back home. She was more excited than ever about the family's plan for a bed-and-breakfast, which was good. The inn's first guests were coming in less than a week!

Things were going well at Miller Farm, too. Even though Grandpa couldn't find the exact latch he had wanted at the hardware store, no ponies had escaped from the field. Grandpa had ordered the new, improved latch, and any day it would arrive in the mail. For now, Grandma and Grandpa used a whole roll of twine to tie the gate shut at night.

But all the knots in the twine made it hard to get the gate open again, and that's just what Willa wanted to do. She, Ben, and Grandma were going on a ride together to celebrate the end of the first week of school. As usual, Willa would ride Starbuck. Ben would ride the big sweetheart Jake, who was an honest-to-goodness real draft horse. The surprise was that instead of walking alongside the horses, Grandma Edna was going to ride too. Even more unexpected was the fact that she intended to ride the new pony, Fancy.

"This pony needs to get out and about," the retired vet said as she pulled herself into the saddle. "Otherwise, she makes plans of her own."

Willa turned around in her saddle and locked eyes with Ben. Ben raised his eyebrows. There Grandma went again, with her mysterious statements. Willa and Ben had attempted to figure them out, but they hadn't had much luck. For now, Grandma said nothing more. She never gave them more than a hint.

From the various murmurs and comments,

Willa and Ben were fairly certain that Grandma Edna blamed Fancy for both escapes, but they didn't know why. As far as they knew, Starbuck was the only pony that had left the farm when the gate was open on the first day of school.

Grandpa Reed wasn't helping them get to the bottom of things either. They had asked him specific questions, but he had not given them specific answers.

Both kids listened closely as they rode along the windy beach with their grandmother. She seemed to be having a conversation with Fancy, but her words were too hushed to understand. To make it even harder to hear, Amos let out giddy barks at a steady beat. The puppy loved being near the horses, and he couldn't help announcing his joy to everyone.

From this stretch of Chincoteague, the wild island of Assateague did not look very far away. It reminded Willa of what Sarah had said. Was it possible that Starbuck wanted to be free again? It pained Willa to think of it. Part of her heart belonged to Starbuck. She wanted the pony to be close to her . . . and Ben.

After a long walk along the beach, they were nearing the farm again. "I dropped my walkie-talkie!" Ben called out as soon as he realized it was missing. "I had it at the start. I swear."

Willa's tummy was already rumbling for dinner. She couldn't imagine having to go back and search for her brother's tech gear. "Why did you take a walkie-talkie on a horseback ride?" she asked, annoyed. He insisted on taking that thing *everywhere*.

"It might have come in handy," he replied.

"Well, a walkie-talkie would be handy now, so we could call someone to go look for it," Willa mumbled.

"Now, children," Grandma Edna began, and they were certain she was about to scold them both, but she was interrupted by a faint jingle. It was a tinkling sound that was growing louder by the second. Soon, it was joined by jolly panting.

"It's Amos!" Ben called. "He has my walkie-talkie!" The puppy was bounding up behind them, his collar clattering with each stride. His sharp puppy teeth clenched Ben's gadget, the antenna sticking up in the air.

"Well, thank goodness," Grandma said. "That pup can track down anything. On Monday he

dug up one of my gardening gloves. I thought it was gone for good."

Amos stopped next to Starbuck, and the pony reached down to nuzzle the puppy. "She's thanking him," Ben noted. The puppy raised his nose and licked Starbuck's muzzle. "They're friends."

Willa was relieved. Between the long school day, the chores at home, and fun at the farm, she was hungry and exhausted. It was good that Amos had found the walkie-talkie. He was earning his keep—and his bike rides.

The topic of the runaway ponies came up again at dinner that night. "Lena thinks that Fancy is some kind of escape artist," Willa shared. "She thinks Fancy is the one who let Starbuck out, that maybe Fancy can pick locks. Remember how she got from one field to the other when both gates were closed?"

"Does Grandma Edna have a secret?" Ben wondered out loud. "Why won't she tell us what is going on? Is it because we're kids?" A pout appeared on Ben's face as he asked the last question.

Mom looked at Dad before she answered. "I don't think Grandma is trying to keep anything from you, at least not on purpose. You know, she often thinks of those horses and ponies like they're family, so she tries not to say mean things about them." Mom lifted a flowered napkin to wipe the corners of her mouth. "And she's never been one to start rumors."

"Rumors about a pony?" Ben said, swallowing a giggle.

"Grandma Edna doesn't like gossip," Mom stated. "She thinks it's a waste of time."

"Well, she's said a whole lot about Fancy," Willa explained. "But it's all under her breath. We can't hear a single word."

"Maybe you'll be able to figure it out next week, when you stay there," Dad suggested.

Mom had planned a lot of last-minute projects for the inn. Dad had suggested that it might be easier for the kids to stay at their grandparents' while the work was being done. As soon as it was complete, the first guests would arrive at the bed-and-breakfast. Willa and Ben would stay over at Grandma and Grandpa's then, too.

Part of Willa was sad to miss the first visitors at Misty Inn. But she knew she and

Ben would have fun at Miller Farm. The best part was that Grandma couldn't send Starbuck to a new home while Willa and Ben were staying there . . . at least not if they had anything to say about it!

Chapter 8

FROM THE BEGINNING, MOM AND DAD HAD SAID that the inn would be a Dunlap Family Adventure. Willa had thought that it would be like the time they drove the car all the way to the Grand Canyon. But the inn felt bigger than the Grand Canyon, if that was possible. Every day there was another closet to clean out, a new paint color to pick, a new recipe to taste. It was a lot, but no project felt bigger than trying to move all the furniture in the house into the kitchen.

"This chair is heeea-vy," Ben groaned, his fingers burning from the weight. Willa could feel the muscles in her arms stretching and straining.

"Kids, kids, put that down," Dad advised, swooping in to help them lower the chair's base. "It's too heavy."

"But there's only heavy stuff left," Willa said.

"Then it'll have to wait for your mom and me," said Dad. "Or the workers tomorrow morning." After the leak on the third floor dribbled all the way down the stairs, the wood floors were splotchy and stained. Mom wanted them to shine. While the floors were being

refinished, all the furniture needed to be somewhere else. It was a big job.

Dad took a quick survey of their progress
and then collapsed onto the chair, right where
they'd dropped it in the middle of the hallway.
"You should go pack, and then I'll take you to
the farm," he said, resting his eyes. "You guys
are lucky you'll get a break from this place."

Willa felt bad for her dad. He was a chef. He
had always been excited about the restaurant
side of the inn, but lately he and Mom had been
thinking about everything else. Handmade
quilts. Fancy brass doorknobs. Online reser-
vations. Antique lamps. "There are only two
people coming to the inn, right?" Willa said. "It
doesn't have to be perfect."

Dad sighed. "When you get older, you'll

realize that in real life, there is no such thing as perfect," he said, his eyes still closed. "But when your mother's involved, it has to be pretty darn close."

Life at Miller Farm seemed much more calm. Even though the kids were spending several nights, Grandma Edna planned to stick to her usual routine. "I'll put you to work," she said. Willa and Ben were happy to help out, especially when it came to tending to Jake and the ponies.

The very first night, they started by mucking manure from the field. Unlike at Misty Inn, the horses and ponies at the rescue center spent the night outside. "More like in the wild," Grandma Edna had insisted as she slung a shovelful into the wheelbarrow. Together the three finished in no time.

"You don't have to tie it so tight," Ben said as Willa wound the twine around the gate several times for good measure. "Even if Fancy bites through the twine and opens the gate, Starbuck won't go anywhere. She'll see us go into the house tonight, and she'll know we are here. She doesn't need to try to find us. Right, girl?" Starbuck, who had been staying close to the kids all evening, heaved a snuffled sigh. "See? She agrees," Ben declared.

Ever since Starbuck stopped the bus on the first day of school, Ben had decided that she had been looking for them. He believed it was the only explanation. "She wanted to find us," Ben said. "You and me."

He was even more convinced the next morning, when all was well in the field. Starbuck, Fancy, Jake, Annie, and every other pony was quietly grazing in the early sun. They were all there when Willa and Ben came home from school as well.

The second week of school had been good for both of them. Sarah and Lena had introduced Willa to several kids, and Willa had started to pick up on Mr. McGory's humor. He was funny! Best of all, Willa had noticed Ben laughing with a group of boys in his gym class. Ben and Chipper still carried their walkie-talkies everywhere, but at least Ben was starting to open up to other kids as well.

"Finally got the right latch," Grandpa announced as the kids walked up the long driveway on Friday afternoon, "so we don't have to deal with that prickly twine anymore." This was good news to Willa, because the twine made her fingers red and itchy. Even better, she wouldn't have to worry about Starbuck getting out anymore. That was one less reason for Grandma Edna to insist on finding a new home for the pony.

That evening the sky was a deep shade of purple. Willa and Ben hoped that all was going well with their parents at home. The first guests should have arrived at Misty Inn. Willa hoped they were enjoying the sunset and all the wonder of being on Chincoteague Island.

At Miller Farm the pastures seemed to be filled with a lavender mist. To Willa and Ben, it felt almost magical, getting to feed Starbuck fresh carrots from the garden just before bed-time. They were in their pajamas and barn boots. It was a funny combination, but it felt good. It felt special.

Both kids were happy to have Buttercup staying in their barn at home, but Butter-cup was not their horse. She belonged to the Starlings, Sarah and Chipper's family. It was different being on Miller Farm at night, spend-ing these lazy hours with Starbuck. Willa and Ben loved Starbuck as if she were their own.

Saying good night to the pony was easier when they knew they would see her first thing in the morning. Even Amos, who usually whim-pered whenever they had to leave the farm, seemed more at ease. Maybe it was because he was allowed to sleep inside when the kids stayed at their grandparents' house. At Misty Inn, he always slept in the barn.

"Sweet dreams, Starbuck," Willa said, turning the latch on the new lock. Ben petted the pony's muzzle and double-checked the gate. Willa picked up Amos and blew Starbuck one last kiss before heading inside for the night.

Willa went to sleep smiling, but she woke up a few hours later. Amos was whining even though his eyes were closed. The puppy had awakened Ben, too. "Poor little guy. He must be having a bad dream," Willa said. Ben rested his hand on Amos's side, and the pup quieted down.

But his whimpers returned a few hours later. "What should we do?" Ben asked as the whining grew louder. The kids' grandparents were sleeping in the next room, and they didn't dare disturb them.

"Maybe we should wake him up," she suggested, but she wasn't certain. "It might stop the dream, and he can go back to sleep."

Both kids crawled out of bed and sat next to Amos. As soon as Ben gave him a shake, the puppy jolted awake. He stopped whining but started barking. Sharp, insistent barks.

"Shhhhh." Willa tried to soothe him, but Amos did not want to be soothed. He jumped up, bolted to the bedroom door, and nudged it open. They could hear his collar jingle as he darted through the house.

"He probably needs to go out," Willa said, grabbing her barn boots. Amos wasn't used to being cooped up all night. "We can let him go to the bathroom and bring him right back in." Ben was just a step behind her. They tried to tiptoe as they ran. They found Amos waiting with his cold nose pressed against the door.

The puppy bounded outside and raced toward the front yard. His barks were louder than they had ever been. He sounded excited and afraid. As soon as they rounded the corner, Willa and Ben knew why. The field gate was wide open, and Starbuck was gone.

Chapter 9

"I TRIPLE-CHECKED THE LOCK," BEN DECLARED.

"I know," Willa said. "I'm not blaming you. Remember, I'm the one who locked it in the first place." They both stared at the field. The night air was thick and wet. Even through the haze, the kids could tell that the pasture was full, except for the one pony they wanted to see most.

Willa stepped forward and relocked the gate. "That's not important now. What's important is finding Starbuck." She glanced around anxiously. "Oh no. Where's Amos?"

First the kids checked the barn. No Amos.

"He's probably one step ahead of us," Ben replied. "He's probably searching for a trail."

Slowly, Willa followed her brother's thinking. She realized that Amos had known all along. Even in his sleep, the puppy had suspected something was wrong. "We have to find him," she said.

Ben straightened up and looked around. The morning was still. "I think I hear him. Behind the house."

Brother and sister rushed to find the puppy, their bare feet loose in their boots. "Amos,"

Willa called in a breathy whisper when they reached the backyard. Amos bounded forward with a yip. He stopped when he reached Willa, and sat down. "That's weird," she said. "He never sits."

Next, the puppy looked longingly into the woods. He sniffed the air, raised one paw, and whimpered.

While the sky around the house was starting to brighten to a dull gray, the wooded area was still dark and moody. "What do you think?" Willa asked.

"I think Amos is good at finding things. Grandma's glove. My walkie-talkie." As he spoke, he touched his hand to the gadget, which was dangling from the waistband of his plaid pajama pants. "And Starbuck," he added hopefully.

The puppy sniffed the air again.

"Okay, Amos," Willa said, ruffling the black patch of fur on his back. "Help us find her."

The puppy turned and trotted toward a gap in the trees. He stopped and smelled, then glanced back. "We're coming," Willa told him, but the shadows were daunting. Once they were under the trees, Willa could barely make out the path ahead of her. "Watch out," she warned Ben. "There are wet leaves on the ground. They're slippery."

Their eyes slowly adjusted, but Willa found she used her hearing more to pick up on Amos's cues: his sniffs, his pants, the upbeat jingle of his collar. He had run ahead, and she caught glimpses of his white tail only now and then.

The moist air clung to her skin, attracting a

chill. She didn't know if her goose bumps were from the cold or her concern.

"I don't get why she left," Ben said after a while. "She knew we were right there. Right in the farmhouse."

Without even looking, Willa could picture the pout on her brother's face. She felt the same way. Why did Starbuck escape? Could Sarah have been right? Did Starbuck want to be free? Willa knew that the wild horses swam the channel from Assateague every year for the pony auction. If Starbuck had made it across the water as a foal, she could certainly do it now as a full-grown pony. What if Amos wasn't on the right path? What if Starbuck was headed for the water? Willa worried that she and Ben might not see their favorite pony again.

Ben kept his eyes focused on Willa's boots. They were yellow and caught the small amount of light that seeped through the trees' leaves. He had to make sure to duck under low limbs, and push branches out of the way. Once, he tripped over a thick root. He hadn't even been able to see it! He wondered how Starbuck could pick her way through these dim woods. And why? The muddy ground was slick. There weren't any appealing patches of grass to eat. She should have just stayed back at Miller Farm. It didn't make any sense.

As Amos and the kids made their way, bird chirps began to announce the morning. Willa could hear the rev of car engines starting up. It was Saturday, so there wouldn't be a lot of traffic, but it didn't make Willa worry less.

There were still plenty of dangers for a lost pony.

Even though they were new to Chincoteague, Ben thought he knew the island fairly well. They had ridden their bikes all over that summer. They had explored the sandy stretches of beach. But Ben had no idea where they were now. At times, it seemed like they were winding through a deep forest. At others, he could make out where the trees came to an end, but what was on the other side? A grassy yard? A hidden cove?

They hadn't seen Amos for a while when a shrill bark cut through the woods. "It's him," Willa said. "He's up ahead."

As they grew nearer, they heard a rustling. It was the sound of a struggle. Willa took quick, short steps, dodging rocks and holes. The path had all but disappeared. They weren't on a proper trail anymore, but Amos had still found what they were looking for. Up ahead, Willa could make out the creamy color of Starbuck's coat.

Amos gave a bark of encouragement just as Willa and Ben ducked under a tree branch to reach them.

"Starbuck, you're caught," Willa said as she approached the startled pony. "Don't you worry. We'll get you out." She ran a hand along the mare's neck, and Starbuck let out a heavy sigh.

"It's a vine," Ben pointed out. "It's between her front legs." He tried to reach for it, but Starbuck pulled away. She shifted, straining against the prickly vine. Her eyes flashed with fear as she realized she was still trapped. Ben stepped back. "It's okay. You're okay."

"We'll figure it out," Willa promised, holding on to the pony's halter. "We'll figure it out," she repeated, but she had no idea how.

Chapter 10

NEITHER WILLA NOR BEN WANTED TO LEAVE Starbuck. Even though morning sunlight was now filtering through the trees, they couldn't see a clear path. They didn't know where they were. It seemed like Starbuck had gone to a lot of trouble to end up in the middle of nowhere.

"We should stick together," Willa said, still

gripping Starbuck's halter. Ben nodded. He now stood at Starbuck's side, using two fingers to rub her neck in tiny circles. The motion seemed to calm her, and it made him feel better too.

Willa was the one who had remembered that Ben had his walkie-talkie, and it came in very handy. Ben buzzed Chipper, who had his walkie-talkie right at his bedside, like a loyal best friend would. Chipper had his dad call Grandma Edna and Grandpa Reed right away.

So all Willa and Ben had to do was wait, and soothe Starbuck, and hope that this wasn't the last straw—the reason that Grandma Edna would insist she needed to find a new home for the pony.

Willa crossed her fingers for luck. She crossed

only one set because Lena had told her that two would cancel each other out. They couldn't have that. They needed all the help they could get. They needed to make sure Starbuck was not leaving Miller Farm.

The two siblings didn't dare talk about punishment, but Ben and Willa were both thinking about it. There had never been a rule against going outside in the tiny hours of the morning and trekking through the woods without telling anyone, but it was kind of obvious that kids shouldn't do that. They were pretty sure they'd get in trouble.

"Willa! Ben! Amos! Starbuck!"

Amos was the first to return Grandma Edna and Grandpa Reed's calls. He did so with three snappy barks.

"We're over here." Willa's call was much softer. She didn't want to startle Starbuck, who had finally settled down.

"Hold tight." Grandpa's voice was gruff and muffled.

"On our way!" Grandma's rang out like a dinner bell.

Ben held his breath as their grandparents appeared through the thick green of the late-summer plants. Their faces were flushed pink. Tiny beads of sweat glistened on their noses.

"Thank goodness," Grandma said when she got a good look at them. "Everyone okay? Anyone hurt?" She set her veterinarian kit on the damp ground and began to make her rounds. She glanced at Ben and offered a reassuring smile, and then she put her hands on either side of Willa's face and gave her a good stare.

"We're fine," Willa said, "but Starbuck is caught. We can't get her loose."

The vet moved her hand to the pony's neck and then down to her leg. "That's a girl," she murmured as she ducked under the mare's belly to figure out just how tangled the pony and the vine had become.

"Could've been a whole lot worse," she announced, straightening up. "Reed, I think this is a job for you and your pocketknife. Kids, you keep Starbuck calm. She needs to be absolutely still."

Grandpa Reed rummaged around and pulled out a knife with a maroon case and lots of slots for blades. Ben scowled when Grandpa unfolded one that was shaped like a small spear. It looked so sharp. Was it safe to use so close to Starbuck?

Grandpa got right to work. "Didn't think I'd be pruning vines at this hour," he said, all hunched over. His arm made short sawing motions. Willa concentrated on petting Starbuck's muzzle. The pony lowered her head, resting it on Willa's shoulder. Willa could feel the warmth of her, and hear the peaceful rhythm of her breath.

After a while Grandpa got down on his knees to go after the piece that was wrapped around Starbuck's hoof. "That just about does it," he announced a few minutes later, pushing himself up with a grunt. "Now, how do we get this pony home?"

"That's just what I was trying to figure out," Grandma Edna replied. "We've got ourselves a rare situation."

Willa felt her heart clench. She had been dreading this moment. She looked over at Ben. His eyes were pinched with worry. They couldn't listen, not if Grandma was going to send Starbuck away.

"It isn't safe to take the trail back to the farm. I'm not sure how that pony made it this far without getting hurt, not to mention the two of you in the dark." Willa and Ben forced themselves to meet their grandma's gaze. Her blue eyes could sometimes appear overly serious, but not now. Now they were soft and sincere.

"We're relieved everyone is all right," Grandpa mumbled in agreement.

"But I think we need to talk about Starbuck getting loose. That's two times now. And we should probably ask ourselves why."

This is it, Willa thought. She bit her lip, preparing herself for bad news.

"I'm not so sure this pony was running away from home," Grandma Edna continued, "as much as she was running *to* one."

Willa and Ben looked at each other, confused.

Grandma Edna spoke again, deliberately. "I think Starbuck is trying to tell us something. I think she's ready for her new home." What was Grandma saying? It was like she was speaking in code. Willa dropped her gaze and studied her boots. They were caked in mud, like Ben's, and her bare feet were sweaty inside. She couldn't believe that they'd tracked Starbuck all the way here and Grandma still wanted to send her to another home.

"But we really love her," Ben said. "We think she's the greatest." Willa nodded in agreement.

"And she feels the same about you," Grandma Edna said.

Hearing this, Willa thought her heart would explode. Why was life so hard? She wrapped her arms around Starbuck's warm neck and let the tears stream down her cheeks.

When she heard a repeated clicking, she looked up. Ugh. Why was Grandma Edna typing on her phone at a time like this? Then she heard a door slam shut. That was odd. Willa had thought they were in the middle of nowhere.

"Willa? Ben?" That was Mom's voice. It was

faint, but Willa knew it was her mother.

"What's Mom doing all the way out here?" she asked Grandma.

Grandma's eyes danced when she smiled. "You kids don't know where we are, do you?"

They both shook their heads.

"You don't think Starbuck would go to all this trouble just to lead you to a dead end, do you?" Grandma joined Willa and Ben, right up close to Starbuck's head. "They underestimated you, girl. Didn't they? They haven't figured it out yet. When they do, they'll be mighty impressed." Starbuck twitched her ears toward Grandma Edna and gave a quick snort in response.

"So where are we?" Ben asked, looking around the thick brush.

"It's like I told you. Starbuck wasn't running away from home, but running to it. Look through those leaves. What do you see?"

Willa squinted where Grandma was pointing. It was hard to see anything against the rising sun.

"Just the sky," Ben answered. "And maybe something white."

"Yes, something white," Grandma agreed. "Let's go."

Grandpa had been busy clearing a path in that very direction. "Watch for those thorny bushes," he warned. "Someone really needs to clean out these overgrown weeds."

As they walked, Willa felt something pricking at her skin. Goose bumps. She gripped Starbuck's halter more tightly, and the pony followed close behind. Ben kept glancing back at them. The plants began to thin, and something came into view. It was a barn. It was red. It looked like any old red barn. But just past the barn was a tall white house, and in front of the house were Mom and Dad.

Willa felt her tears return. How could Starbuck have possibly known where they lived? She couldn't. It was as plain as that. But here they were.

When Willa realized that Mom and Dad were in their nicest pajamas, she realized that Misty Inn had guests. The visiting couple had come out on the porch. Willa was certain they were admiring Starbuck. The Chincoteague pony lifted her head high, looking noble and wise.

The family all met and there were hugs for everyone. Dad knelt down to give Amos a pet. Mom brushed the hair from Willa's face and smiled. Ben went back to rubbing Starbuck's neck. No one really said anything, and Willa still felt confused and a little afraid. She was grateful when Ben finally spoke up.

"Is this real?" he asked.

The adults all laughed. "Yes," Mom said. Dad's arm was wrapped around her. "It only seems fitting for Misty Inn to have its very own Chincoteague pony."

"Starbuck just insisted on hurrying things up," Grandma explained.

"And that troublemaker Fancy was all too willing to help," Grandpa added. "Those two were in cahoots from the start."

Willa and Ben shared expressions of disbelief. It seemed impossible.

Grandma tickled the whiskers on Starbuck's lip as she spoke. "It's true. Fancy had a history of opening gates at her old home, but I doubt she'll be opening any more. I think she made her point."

So the adults assumed that Starbuck had been plotting to come live at Misty Inn all along? And that Fancy, the expert lock picker, had been in on the plan? It sounded so far-fetched. Had the adults really convinced themselves it was true? They acted as if the kids should have known that Starbuck would soon live there, that Starbuck would soon be their own.

Willa knew her friends would never believe it. She told herself it didn't matter. Somehow, they were all safe. And they were home.

Standing with everyone in a circle in the driveway, Willa felt the warmth of being surrounded by family. She smiled at Ben and felt the comfort of being understood. She placed her hand on Starbuck's face and felt the happiness of belonging, because they all belonged to one another. They were meant to be together, even when it wasn't that easy.

Willa promised herself she would remember this moment. She recalled how Dad had said that in real life, nothing was perfect. Willa suspected that Dad was right, but, deep in her heart, she knew that this was pretty darn close.

ABOUT THE SERIES

Marguerite Henry's Misty Inn series is inspired by the award-winning books by Marguerite Henry, the beloved author of such classic horse stories as *King of the Wind*; *Misty of Chincoteague*; *Justin Morgan Had a Horse*; *Stormy, Misty's Foal*; *Misty's Twilight*, and *Album of Horses*, among many other titles.

Learn more about the world of Marguerite Henry at www.MistyofChincoteague.com.